The Moon-Bog

*A Lovecraftian Tale of Ancient Curses
and Haunting Horror*

A Modern Translation

Adapted for the Contemporary Reader

H.P. Lovecraft

Translated by Tim Zengerink

Table of Contents

Preface - Message to the Reader

What If You Could Help Rebuild the Greatest Library in Human History?

Thousands of years ago, the Library of Alexandria stood as the crown jewel of human achievement — a sanctuary where the collected wisdom of every known civilization was gathered, preserved, and shared freely.

And then, it was lost.

Through fire, conquest, and the slow erosion of time, humanity lost not just books — but ideas, dreams, discoveries, and stories that could have changed the world forever.

Today, the Library of Alexandria lives again — and you are invited to be a part of its restoration.

Our mission is simple yet profound:

To rebuild the greatest library the world has ever known, and to translate all timeless works into every language and dialect, so that no seeker of knowledge is ever left behind again.

By joining our movement to rebuild the modern Library of Alexandria, you become part of an unprecedented mission:

- **Unlimited Access to the Greatest Audiobooks & eBooks Ever Written:**

  Instantly explore thousands of legendary works—Plato, Shakespeare, Jane Austen, Leo Tolstoy, and countless more. All instantly available to read or listen, placing a complete literary universe at your fingertips.

- **Beautiful Paperback & Deluxe Editions at Printing Cost**

  Own any title as an elegant paperback, deluxe hardcover, or stunning collectible boxset—offered to you at true printing cost, delivered straight to your door. Build your personal Library of Alexandria, crafted for beauty, built for durability, and worthy of proud display.

- **Fresh Translations for Modern Readers—in Every Language & Dialect**

  Enjoy timeless masterpieces reimagined in clear, contemporary language—no more outdated phrases or obscure references. Alongside the original versions, we're tirelessly translating these classics into every language and dialect imaginable, ensuring accessibility and understanding across cultures and generations.

- **Join a Global Renaissance of Literature & Knowledge**

  You directly support expanding our library, publishing deluxe editions at true cost, translating works into all global languages, and bringing humanity's greatest stories to people everywhere. By joining today, you're not just preserving a legacy of masterpieces; you set in motion a powerful wave of literary accessibility.

Become a Torchbearer of Knowledge.

Join us for free now at **LibraryofAlexandria.com**

Together, we will ensure that the light of human wisdom never fades again.

With gratitude and a shared love of knowledge,

The Modern Library of Alexandria Team

Visit:

www.libraryofalexandria.com

Or scan the code below:

Introduction

Greed, Superstition,
and the Ancient Curse of the Land

H.P. Lovecraft's "The Moon-Bog," originally penned in 1921 and published in the March 1926 issue of Weird Tales, stands as a potent example of the author's early experimentation with classical Gothic tropes woven together with folkloric horror. Unlike Lovecraft's more expansive cosmic tales such as "The Call of Cthulhu" or "At the Mountains of Madness," this story belongs to a more earthbound category, one where myth, landscape, and hubris collide in a cautionary tale steeped in revenge, decay, and the haunting persistence of ancient ways.

Set in an unspecified region of Ireland, "The Moon-Bog" tells the story of an American landowner named Denys Barry, who purchases a parcel of ancestral land in the Old World and attempts to modernize it by draining a swampy bog to make way for civilization. His goal is development, but his efforts come at the cost of disturbing sacred ground—land believed by locals to be the resting place of long-dead druids and their sacrificial victims. Though warned by the superstitious locals, Barry dismisses their fears, choosing instead to press forward with his plans. The locals flee. The laborers refuse to continue. But Barry persists—until the bog itself rises to consume him, and the ancient dead exact their vengeance beneath the light of a full moon.

Told through the eyes of an unnamed narrator who survives the ordeal, the story unfolds in a manner that emphasizes atmosphere over explanation. The horror is gradual, vague, and all the more unsettling for it. Lovecraft leans into the traditional fear of marshes as liminal spaces—neither land nor water, known nor unknown. The bog, in his hands, becomes not just a place but a presence. It seeps into the narrative as something alive, aware, and waiting. Beneath its soft soil lies a memory so old that time has forgotten it, but not erased it.

"The Moon-Bog" is notable for its grounding in folklore and its subtle critique of colonial arrogance. Denys Barry's attempts to impose order and rationality on a land with its own deep memory mirrors the hubris of many Lovecraftian protagonists—men who believe that knowledge, wealth, or science can master all things. But in this story, the punishment is not meted out by cosmic entities or alien gods. It comes from the land itself. From its history. From its silence. And when that silence is broken, the consequences are swift and absolute.

Druidic Echoes, Landscape Horror, and the Death of Rationality

What distinguishes "The Moon-Bog" from many of Lovecraft's other stories is its overt use of European folklore and its engagement with themes of pagan tradition and natural retribution. While Lovecraft frequently invents his own mythologies, in this tale he draws on a more traditional European Gothic heritage: druidic sacrificial rites, moonlit marshes, and the uncanny knowledge possessed by local peasants. These elements coalesce into a story that feels at once familiar and deeply unsettling, like an old tale told by the fire that leaves more questions than answers.

The bog is not merely a geographic feature—it is the grave of an ancient culture, and in Lovecraft's hands, it functions as a vessel of memory and wrath. Marshes and swamps have long been associated in folklore with spirits, curses, and bodies that do not stay buried. Their very nature—unpredictable, sinking, and impenetrable—makes them ideal settings for horror. In "The Moon-Bog," the landscape is more than a backdrop; it is an antagonist. It watches, it remembers, and it retaliates.

Denys Barry's downfall is sealed the moment he ignores the voices of those who understand the land better than he does. Lovecraft's story plays upon the tension between ancient superstition and modern progress, between the known and the instinctual. The villagers and workers sense the danger. They feel it. But Barry, with his rational mind and capitalist ambition, ignores these signals. This tension is not just thematic—it is structural. The story begins with Barry's confidence and ends with his erasure. He is not merely killed—he is swallowed by the very land he tried to conquer.

Lovecraft's prose in this tale is rich and evocative, using sensory details to draw the reader into the oppressive dampness and lunar eeriness of the bog. The slow build-up of tension, the descriptions of half-seen figures rising from the mist, and the final descent into dream-like horror all serve to reinforce the story's central idea: that the past is not dead, and that places hold memory. The bog is not cursed because of a single event—it is cursed because memory itself lingers, staining the earth like blood that can never be washed away.

The use of the moon as a symbol is equally significant. The moon has long been associated with madness, transformation, and liminality. It is a celestial observer, often indifferent and distant, yet in folklore it is also a trigger—marking times of ritual, awakening the dead, illuminating secrets. In "The Moon-Bog," it serves as the final catalyst. When the moonlight reveals the forms rising from the bog, it is not just a lighting device. It is a summoning. It marks the hour of judgment.

This modern edition has been revised for clarity while preserving the cadence and rhythm of Lovecraft's original style. Archaic phrasing has been lightly modernized, and sentence structures have been streamlined for readability without losing the weight and atmosphere of the original prose. The story's effect lies not in direct shocks, but in suggestion—in mood, implication, and the slow, sinking realization that something old and angry has been disturbed.

To read "The Moon-Bog" is to enter a world where the ground remembers, where superstition is not ignorance but wisdom in disguise, and where the past is not behind us, but beneath us—waiting to rise. It is a story that warns not of distant stars or ancient aliens, but of what happens when we forget that the earth itself holds power. In this tale, horror does not come from space or from dreams, but from roots, from tradition, and from a silence that is not empty, but expectant. The terror beneath the marsh is not just ancient—it is patient. And when it returns, it does so not with rage, but with the cold inevitability of nature reclaiming what was never truly lost.

The Moon-Bog

No one knows exactly where Denys Barry went, or what strange and frightening place he might have ended up in. I was with him the last night he was seen, and I heard him scream when something came for him. But even though the people and police of County Meath searched far and wide, they never found him—or the others. Now, whenever I hear frogs croaking in the swamps or see the moon shining in lonely places, I can't help but shiver.

I had known Denys Barry back in America, where he had become wealthy. I was happy for him when he bought back his family's old castle near the bog in the quiet town of Kilderry. His father had come from there, and Denys wanted to enjoy his success in the place his ancestors once ruled. A long time ago, his family had built the castle and lived in it, but it had been empty and falling apart for generations. After moving to Ireland, Barry often wrote to me, saying how he was restoring the gray stone castle tower by tower. He told me how the ivy was growing back over the walls, just like in the old days, and how the local people were thankful he had returned with his fortune. But eventually, things changed. The people stopped thanking him and started leaving instead, as if something terrible had happened. That's when he sent me a letter asking me to visit, saying he was lonely in the castle with only the new workers and servants he had brought from the north.

It turned out the bog was at the center of all the trouble, as Barry explained the night I arrived. I had come to Kilderry one summer evening as the sun was setting. The sky was golden, the hills and forests were green, and the bog was a deep blue. On a small island in the middle of the swamp, I saw some strange old ruins glowing in the fading light. It was a beautiful scene—but the villagers in Ballylough had warned me not to go. They said Kilderry was cursed. I felt uneasy when I saw the castle's towers lit up by the fiery sunset. Barry had sent his car to meet me at the train station since Kilderry didn't have its own rail line. The locals avoided both the car and the driver from the north, but when they saw I was heading to the castle, they gave me nervous looks and whispered warnings. That night, after we reunited, Barry told me everything.

The people of Kilderry had left because Barry was planning to drain the large bog. Even though he loved Ireland, his time in America had changed him. He didn't see the bog as something beautiful, but as wasted space where useful land could be made. He didn't care about the old legends and superstitions tied to it, and he laughed when the locals refused to help with the project. But when they saw he was serious, they cursed him and left, taking their few belongings to Ballylough. He hired workers from the north instead, and replaced the servants who had quit. Still, he felt isolated among strangers—so he invited me to come.

When I heard what had scared the villagers away, I laughed just as Barry had. Their fears were vague, strange, and sounded completely ridiculous. They told stories about a strange spirit guarding the bog, living in the ruined buildings on the small island I had seen. They talked about ghostly lights that appeared during moonless nights, cold winds on warm evenings, and white ghost-like figures floating over the water. Some even believed a hidden stone city lay deep below the swamp. But the main fear, which every single villager agreed on, was that anyone who tried to disturb or drain the red, mossy bog would bring a terrible curse upon themselves. The old men said the bog hid ancient secrets that had been buried since the time of the plague that struck the children of Partholan—mythical people who were said to have come from Greece long before recorded history. While ancient writings say they were buried elsewhere, the elders in Kilderry believed one city had been forgotten, watched over only by its moon goddess, and hidden under the forest-covered hills when a different tribe arrived from Scythia in their ships.

These were the strange tales that caused the villagers to abandon Kilderry. And once I heard them, I understood why Barry didn't believe them. In fact, he was fascinated by old ruins and had planned to study the bog's secrets once it was drained. He had already visited the white ruins on the island many times. They were clearly ancient, and their shape was different from most ruins in Ireland, but they were too broken down to say much about their history. Now that the drainage work was about to start, the northern workers were getting ready to strip the bog of its moss and heather. They would soon destroy the small, shell-lined streams and peaceful blue pools surrounded by reeds.

After Barry told me everything, I felt really tired. The day's travels had worn me out, and he had stayed up talking late into the night. A servant led me to my room, which was in a far-off tower of the castle. From my window, I could see the quiet village rooftops, now home to the northern workers, the old parish church with its tall spire, and far out across the bog, the ancient ruins on the small island—glowing pale and ghostly in the moonlight. Just as I started to fall asleep, I thought I heard soft, strange sounds in the distance. They were wild and kind of musical, stirring something strange inside me that colored my dreams. But when I woke up the next morning, it all felt like a dream. What I had imagined in my sleep was more amazing than any music I might have heard.

Influenced by the stories Barry had told, I had dreamed of a beautiful ancient city in a green valley. There were marble streets, statues, villas, temples, carvings, and writing—all reminding me of ancient Greece. When I told Barry about my dream, we both laughed. I laughed harder, though, because he seemed puzzled by something else: the workers from the north had all overslept again. For the sixth time, they had gotten up slowly and groggily, acting like they hadn't slept well—even though everyone knew they had gone to bed early.

That morning and afternoon, I walked through the sunlit village on my own. Barry was busy with final plans to start draining the bog, so I talked now and then with some of the idle workers. They didn't seem happy. Most of them looked uneasy, like they had had strange dreams they couldn't remember clearly. I told them about my dream, and they didn't react—until I mentioned the weird sounds I thought I'd heard. Then they looked at me strangely and said they remembered hearing odd sounds too.

That evening, Barry had dinner with me and said the draining would begin in two days. I was glad in a way, even though I didn't like the idea of destroying the moss, heather, and peaceful streams and pools. Still, my curiosity was growing. I wanted to know what ancient secrets might be buried in the thick layers of peat. But that night, my usual dreams of flute music and marble buildings ended suddenly and uneasily. In the dream, a horrible plague hit the city in the valley, and then a massive landslide from the forested hills buried the streets and the dead—leaving only the temple of Artemis untouched at the top of the hill, where the moon-priestess Cleis lay cold and still, wearing an ivory crown on her silver hair.

I said I woke up suddenly, and in fear. At first, I couldn't tell if I was awake or dreaming, because I could still hear the sharp, strange sound of flutes. But then I saw the moonlight on the floor and the shadowed shapes of the old window, and I knew I was in my room at the castle. Then, from far away, I heard a clock strike two, and I knew for sure I was awake. But the music kept going—that strange, distant piping that made me think of mythical creatures dancing in the woods. I couldn't sleep, so I got up and paced the room. By chance, I looked out the north window at the quiet village and the plain beside the bog. I hadn't meant to look outside—I just needed to distract myself from the music.

But what I saw there is something I'll never forget.

In the moonlight that covered the plain, I saw a strange and silent scene. To the sound of those haunting pipes, a crowd of moving figures drifted across the field. They swayed and spun in a dance that reminded me of some ancient festival—something that might have been done in honor of a goddess during a harvest moon in old Sicily. The open space, the moonlight, the moving shadows, and the music all together created a vision so eerie it nearly froze me. Even though I was afraid, I noticed something that made it worse—half of those dancing were the workers I had thought were asleep in bed. The rest were ghostly, pale beings dressed in white—unclear and misty, like water spirits or nymphs from the bog. I don't know how long I stood there watching from the tower window before I suddenly fainted and fell into a deep, dreamless sleep. The bright sun woke me the next morning.

My first thought was to tell Barry everything I had seen and heard. But once I saw the morning sunlight shining through the window, I convinced myself it had all just been a dream. I tend to imagine strange things, but I'm not someone who usually believes in them. So instead, I talked to the workers, who had slept in again and didn't remember anything from the night before— just hazy dreams about high-pitched sounds. The memory of the strange music stuck with me all day. I even wondered if the autumn crickets had arrived early and were making people dream strange things.

Later in the day, I watched Barry in the library. He was deeply focused on his plans for the draining project, which would start the next day. For the first time, I felt a bit of the same fear the villagers must have felt. I couldn't explain why, but I was nervous about disturbing the old bog and whatever lay beneath its dark, quiet surface. I imagined terrible things hidden under layers of peat, buried for who knows how long. Digging them up didn't seem like a good idea. I even thought about finding a reason to leave the castle. I casually brought it up with Barry, but when he laughed it off so loudly, I dropped the subject. So I stayed silent as the sun set in glowing reds and golds behind the hills, and Kilderry looked like it was burning in the light—like a warning from something ancient.

I'll never know if what happened that night was real or just a dream. It felt far beyond anything natural, yet there's no normal way to explain what happened— especially the disappearances everyone knew about afterward. I went to bed early, feeling uneasy, and couldn't fall asleep for a long time because the tower was so quiet. It was very dark. The sky was clear, but the moon was low and wouldn't rise until early morning. I kept thinking about Denys Barry and what might happen when the bog was drained. I even felt like running outside, taking Barry's car, and driving far away to Ballylough, away from that cursed land. But before I could act on my fear, I fell asleep. I dreamed again of that city in the valley, silent and cold, covered in a terrifying shadow.

It was probably the high-pitched music that woke me, but it wasn't the first thing I noticed. I was lying with my back to the window that looked east over the bog, where the moon would rise. I expected to see soft moonlight on the wall ahead—but the light I saw wasn't from the moon. Instead, a harsh, red glow lit up the room. It wasn't like any light I'd seen before. The beam that came through the Gothic window was intense and unearthly. The whole room was glowing with this strange red light.

I didn't react the way you might expect. Instead of running to the window to see what it was, I panicked and looked away. I fumbled to get dressed, thinking only of escape. I grabbed my gun and hat, but in the end, I lost both—never even using one or wearing the other. At some point, curiosity beat out fear, and I crept toward the glowing window. The awful piping sound still filled the castle and the village as I looked out.

Over the bog, a bright, blood-red light poured from the ruins on the far island. I can't describe how the ruins looked—they didn't seem broken anymore, but whole, massive, shining like marble and stretching tall into the sky. The whole scene felt unreal, like some ancient temple had returned to life. Flutes screamed, drums started to beat, and I thought I saw dark, dancing shapes moving in front of the glowing building. The effect was so overwhelming I might've kept watching forever—until I heard the music grow louder from the other side of the room.

Shaking, filled with fear and wonder, I crossed the room to the north window. From there I could see the village and the plain next to the bog. What I saw next was just as disturbing. In the red light, strange white figures glided and floated slowly across the plain. They were moving in weird, dance-like patterns, like part of an ancient ritual. Their arms waved in time with the eerie flute music, and behind them came the laborers—stumbling blindly, like puppets being pulled by something invisible.

Then, even more figures emerged from the castle, walking like sleepwalkers across the courtyard, through the village, and onto the plain. I recognized them right away—they were Barry's servants from the north. Even the cook was there, his big shape sadly familiar now in this nightmare. The drums pounded, the flutes screamed, and I watched as the white figures—the bog spirits, maybe—slid into the water, vanishing one by one. The workers followed, splashing after them into the bog. When the last one, the fat cook, sank out of sight in a mess of small, bubbling ripples, the drums and flutes stopped, and the red light snapped off instantly. The moon had just risen, but it lit only a quiet, empty village.

I was overwhelmed—shocked, confused, unsure if I was dreaming or awake. I felt frozen, unable to move. I think I started praying, mumbling names from old myths—Artemis, Demeter, Pluto—like I had somehow fallen into an ancient curse. I felt like I'd just witnessed the end of an entire village and was now trapped in the castle with Denys Barry, whose boldness had brought this doom. Thinking of him made me panic even more, and I collapsed on the floor—not unconscious, but completely paralyzed. Then I felt a cold wind coming in through the east window, and I started to hear screams from deep inside the castle.

The screams grew louder and more horrifying. I can't even describe the sound—it still makes me sick to think of it. All I can say is that it came from someone I had once called a friend.

At some point, the freezing wind and terrifying noise must have shocked me into action. The next thing I remember, I was running through the dark hallways, across the castle's courtyard, and into the night. They found me at sunrise, wandering without direction near Ballylough. But what finally broke my mind wasn't what I had seen in the castle or on the plain.

What haunted me—what I kept muttering about— were two strange moments from my escape. First, as I ran along the edge of the bog, I heard a new sound. It was familiar, but wrong. The waters, which had been lifeless, were now alive with giant, slimy frogs. They croaked in sharp, shrill tones that didn't match their size. Under the moonlight, they looked huge and wet, staring up at the sky.

I followed the gaze of one especially large, ugly frog—and that's when I saw the second thing that shattered my sanity.

From the ancient ruins on the island, a pale, flickering beam stretched upward toward the moon. It had no reflection in the water, and along that glowing path I imagined a thin shadow rising—a twisted shape wriggling upward, as if being pulled by something I couldn't see. Even in my madness, I thought the shape looked horribly familiar. It was like a distorted, sick version of someone I once knew.

It looked like Denys Barry.

The End

Thank You for Reading

Dear Reader,

We hope this timeless classic has sparked your imagination and enriched your literary journey. Now that you've turned the final page, we want to share a vision for the future of reading—one where every classic you've ever wanted to explore is at your fingertips, in a format that best suits your life.

We'd like to invite you to gain immediate, unlimited digital & audiobook access to hundreds of the most treasured literary classics ever written—along with the option to secure deluxe paperback, hardcover & box set editions at printing cost. Together, we can spark a new global literary renaissance alongside our small, independent publishing house called "The Library of Alexandria."

Thousands of years ago, the Library of Alexandria stood as a beacon of knowledge—until it was lost to history. We aim to reignite that spirit of preservation and discovery right now, in the modern age—only this time, it's accessible to all, in every language and every format.

Picture a world where every timeless classic, novel, poem, or philosophical treatise is not only available to read but also updated for today's readers—modernized, translated into any language or dialect, and ready to enjoy in any format you choose, whether that is in an eBook, audiobook, paperback, or deluxe hardcover & box set version a printing cost.

By joining our movement to rebuild the modern Library of Alexandria, you become part of an unprecedented mission to offer:

- **Unlimited Audiobook & eBook Access to the Greatest Classics of All Time**

  Instantly explore thousands of legendary works, from Plato and Shakespeare to Jane Austen and Leo Tolstoy. All are instantly ready to read or listen to, giving you a complete literary universe at your fingertips.

- **Paperback & Deluxe Editions at Printing Costs:**

  Purchase any title in a paperback, deluxe hardbound, or deluxe boxset edition at printing costs, shipped right to your doorstep. Curate your personal library of Alexandria with editions worthy of display— crafted to last, designed to captivate, and delivered straight to your door.

- **Modern translations for Contemporary Readers in all languages and dialects**

  Discover a vast selection of classics reimagined in clear, current language—no more struggling with outdated phrases or obscure references. Next to the original versions, we aim to offer translations in as many languages and dialects as possible.

  As we continue our translation efforts and add new languages, readers everywhere can connect with these works as if they were written today. By bridging linguistic divides, you're contributing to ensuring that these timeless stories become more meaningful, accessible, and inspiring for people across the globe.

- **Your Personal Library of Alexandria:**

  Over the months and years, you'll curate a unique physical archive of classics—each volume a testament to your taste, curiosity, and love of knowledge. It's not just about owning books—it's about curating a cultural legacy you'll cherish and pass down for generations to come.

- **Join a Global Literary Renaissance:**

  Your support fuels an ongoing mission: allowing us to reinvest in offering deluxe print editions (including special boxsets) at their true cost, broaden the range of available formats and translations, and extend the reach of these works to new audiences worldwide. By joining today, you're not just preserving a legacy of masterpieces; you set in motion a powerful wave of literary accessibility.

We are more than a publisher—we're a movement, and we can't do it alone. Your support lets us scale our mission, preserving and reimagining history's greatest works for tomorrow's readers.

Become a Torchbearer of knowledge.

Thank you for picking up this book and allowing us into your literary journey. As you turn the pages, know that you're part of something larger: a global effort to keep these stories alive, share their wisdom across borders and generations, and spark a true cultural revival for the modern era.

If this resonates with you—please consider taking the next step by visiting:

www.libraryofalexandria.com

With gratitude and a shared love of knowledge,

The Modern Library of Alexandria Team

Visit:

www.libraryofalexandria.com

Or scan the code below: